13

KT-447-835

Dubliners

Snow was falling in every part of Ireland. It was falling, it seemed for the last time, on the living and the dead.

In these six stories, James Joyce describes the lives of the ordinary people of Dublin, Ireland's capital city, in the early nineteen hundreds. Their lives are often difficult: the world is hard to understand and mistakes are easy to make – they can change your life for ever.

But the people of Dublin are just like people everywhere – the living and the dead.

James Joyce was born in Dublin in 1882 and grew up there. But he grew to dislike the city and left it in 1904 to live in Italy, where he worked as an English teacher. He returned to Ireland only once, in 1912. But Dublin was the only place he ever wrote about. *Dubliners* (1914) was his second book.

The way Joyce wrote was quite new for its time and he could not easily sell his novels and stories. The real people of Dublin did not like *Dubliners*. His great novels *Ulysses* (1922) and *Finnegan's Wake* (1939) were very difficult books. He got almost no money for his writing during his lifetime. He died in 1941, in Zurich, Switzerland.

OTHER TITLES IN THE SERIES

Level 1
Girl Meets Boy
The Hen and the Bull
The Medal of Brigadier Gerard

Level 2
The Birds
Chocky
Don't Look Now
Emily
The Fox
The Ghost of Genny Castle
Grandad's Eleven
The Lady in the Lake
Money to Burn
Persuasion
The Railway Children
The Room in the Tower and Other
    Ghost Stories
Simply Suspense
Treasure Island
Under the Greenwood Tree

Level 3
Black Beauty
The Black Cat and Other Stories
The Book of Heroic Failures
A Catskill Eagle
The Darling Buds of May
Detective Work
Earthdark
Jane Eyre
King Solomon's Mines
Madame Doubtfire
The Man with Two Shadows and
    Other Ghost Stories
Mrs Dalloway
My Family and Other Animals
Rain Man
The Reluctant Queen
Sherlock Holmes and the Mystery
    of Boscombe Pool
The Thirty-nine Steps
Time Bird
Twice Shy

Level 4
The Boys from Brazil
The Breathing Method
The Danger
The Doll's House and Other Stories
Dracula
Far from the Madding Crowd
Farewell, My Lovely
Glitz
Gone with the Wind, Part 1
Gone with the Wind, Part 2
The House of Stairs
The Locked Room and Other
    Horror Stories
The Mill on the Floss
The Mosquito Coast
The Picture of Dorian Gray
Strangers on a Train
White Fang

Level 5
The Baby Party and Other Stories
The Body
The Firm
The Grass is Singing
Jude the Obscure
The Old Jest
The Pelican Brief
Pride and Prejudice
Prime Suspect
A Twist in the Tale
The Warden
Web

Level 6
The Edge
The Long Goodbye
Misery
Mrs Packletide's Tiger and Other
    Stories
The Moonstone
Presumed Innocent
A Tale of Two Cities
The Thorn Birds
Wuthering Heights

Dubliners

JAMES JOYCE

Level 3

Retold by Joc Potter and Andy Hopkins
Series Editor: Derek Strange

PENGUIN BOOKS

PENGUIN BOOKS

Published by the Penguin Group
Penguin Books Ltd, 27 Wrights Lane, London, W8 5TZ, England
Penguin Books USA Inc., 375 Hudson Street, New York, New York 10014, USA
Penguin Books Australia Ltd, Ringwood, Victoria, Australia
Penguin Books Canada Ltd, 10 Alcorn Avenue, Toronto, Ontario, Canada M4V 3B2
Penguin Books (NZ) Ltd, 182–190 Wairau Road, Auckland 10, New Zealand

Penguin Books Ltd, Registered Offices: Harmondsworth, Middlesex, England

First published in 1914
This adaptation published by Penguin Books 1993
2 4 6 8 10 9 7 5 3

Text copyright © Joc Potter and Andy Hopkins 1993
Illustrations copyright © Piers Sandford 1993
All rights reserved

The moral right of the adapters and of the illustrator has been asserted

Illustrations by Piers Sandford

Printed in England by Clays Ltd, St Ives plc
Set in 11/14 pt Lasercomp Bembo

To the teacher:

In addition to all the language forms of Levels One and Two, which are used again at this level of the series, the main verb forms and tenses used at Level Three are:

- past continuous verbs, present perfect simple verbs, conditional clauses (using the 'first' or 'open future' conditional), question tags and further common phrasal verbs
- modal verbs: *have (got) to* and *don't have to* (to express obligation), *need to* and *needn't* (to express necessity), *could* and *was able to* (to describe past ability), *could* and *would* (in offers and polite requests for help), and *shall* (for future plans, offers and suggestions).

Also used are:

- relative pronouns: *who*, *that* and *which* (in defining clauses)
- conjunctions: *if* and *since* (for time or reason), *so that* (for purpose or result) and *while*
- indirect speech (questions)
- participle clauses.

Specific attention is paid to vocabulary development in the Vocabulary Work exercises at the end of the book. These exercises are aimed at training students to enlarge their vocabulary systematically through intelligent reading and effective use of a dictionary.

To the student:

Dictionary Words:

- When you read this book, you will find that some words are darker black than the others on the page. Look them up in your dictionary, if you do not already know them, or try to guess the meaning of the words first, without a dictionary.

Dubliners

An Encounter   7

Eveline   13

The Boarding House   17

Counterparts   21

A Painful Case   26

The Dead   32

An Encounter

Joe Dillon told us about the Wild West. He had a small library of picture books, and every evening we met in Joe's back garden for Indian fights. Joe and his fat brother Leo always won; he was older than many of us and wilder. At the same time I stopped studying because I did not want to seem too interested in school. Then our history teacher, Father Butler, saw Leo Dillon reading a Wild West picture book in class and Leo got into trouble. The Wild West was suddenly less interesting when I saw Leo's fat, worried face.

But I was bored at school and soon I was bored too by our evening fights. I wanted real adventures and you did not find real adventures at home. The summer holidays were near when, with Leo Dillon and a boy called Mahony, I decided to miss a day's school. Each of us saved sixpence and I took all the money.

The night before, I was too excited to sleep. In the morning I was the first at our meeting-place. I hid my books in the long grass at the end of the garden and hurried along by the river. Then I sat and watched the horses; they were pulling business people up the hill. There were tall trees on each side of the street, and the sun shone through them on to the water. I was very happy.

After five or ten minutes, Mahony arrived in his grey suit. We waited together for another quarter of an hour, but Leo Dillon did not come. Mahony, at last, jumped up.

'Come on. Let's go.'

'And his sixpence ..?' I said.

'That's ours now,' said Mahony.

We walked along the North Strand Road and then turned to the right into Wharf Road. Mahony began to play the Indian. First he ran after some girls and then after some small boys who were throwing stones at us. We laughed at Leo Dillon, bored at school because he was frightened to be with us.

We watched while men carried things on and off the boats, and we thought about running away to sea on one of the big ships.

We arrived at the big river. It was busy and noisy with the sound of machines and people shouting. We watched while men carried things on and off the boats, and we thought about running away to sea on one of the big ships. When the workers stopped to eat, we bought some food and had our lunch too. We forgot about school and home; they did not seem important now.

We paid our money to cross the Liffey * in a small boat. When we landed, we watched the sailors taking wood off a Norwegian ship. I looked carefully at the eyes of the foreign sailors because I had the idea that foreign eyes were green. But the sailors' eyes were blue and grey and sometimes black. The only man with green eyes was a tall man who everyone found amusing.

'All right!' he called when a piece of wood fell. 'All right!'

When we were tired of watching, we walked slowly into Ringsend and bought a bottle of pink lemonade each. Mahony ran after a cat, but the cat escaped into a wide field. We followed it for a time. Then we lay in the field and rested.

We were the only people there until a man arrived. I held a piece of grass between my teeth and watched him. He was holding a **stick** in one hand and hitting the ground with it lightly while he walked. He wore an old greenish-black suit and a tall hat. He was not young; his moustache was grey. When he got close to us, he looked at us quickly and then continued on his way. We followed him with our eyes, and after a few minutes he turned round and came back. He walked very slowly, always hitting the ground with his stick – so slowly that he seemed to be looking for something in the grass.

He stopped at our feet and said good-day. We answered him and he sat down slowly and carefully. He began to talk about the weather and then about his schooldays. His words bored us a little and so we kept silent. Then he started to talk about books, about the works of Thomas Moore, Sir Walter Scott and Lord Lytton. My face looked interested, and in the end he said to me:

* *Liffey*. The name of the river that runs through Dublin into the Irish Sea.

9

'Ah, it's clear that you like books too. Now,' he continued, pointing at Mahony's open eyes, 'he's different; he enjoys games. You know, I have all Sir Walter Scott's works and Lord Lytton's works at home. I read them again and again. Of course,' he said, 'there are some of Lord Lytton's books which boys cannot read.'

'Why?' asked Mahony. His question made me uncomfortable. I was not as stupid as Mahony, and the man did not know that. But he only smiled. I could see his yellow teeth.

'Which of you has the most girlfriends?' he asked.

'I've got three,' Mahony said quickly.

'And you?' the man asked.

'None,' I answered. He did not believe me.

'Tell us,' said Mahony, 'how many have you got?'

The man smiled again.

'When I was your age, I had a lot of girlfriends. Every boy has a little girlfriend.'

These words were surprising for an older person. In my heart I agreed with them, but I did not like the sound of them in his mouth. Then he began to speak to us about girls.

'There is nothing I like better than looking at a nice young girl, at her nice white hands and her beautiful soft hair.' He spoke in a low voice, like somebody who is telling secrets. He repeated these words again and again. I looked and listened.

After a long time he stopped and stood up slowly.

'I must leave you for a minute or two,' he said. He walked slowly away from us towards the end of the field. We were silent after he left. Then I heard Mahony's voice:

'I say! Look what he's doing!'

I did not answer or lift my eyes from the ground, so Mahony said again:

'I say... He's a strange one!'

'If he asks us our names,' I said, 'you're Murphy and I'm Smith.'

We said nothing more to each other. I was thinking about leaving when the man came back and sat down with us again. Then Mahony saw the cat. He jumped up and ran across the field

After a long time he stopped and stood up slowly.
'I must leave you for a minute or two,' he said.

after it. The man and I watched. The cat escaped on to a wall, and Mahony began to throw stones at it.

'Your friend is a very wild boy,' the man said after a few minutes of this. 'Do they often hit him at school?'

I stayed silent. They almost never hit people at our school. He started to talk about hitting boys in the same way as he talked before about girls.

'You have to hit boys of that kind and hit them hard. It's the only thing that they understand. Not on the hand or on the ear, but hard, on their bottom.'

I was surprised that his feelings about this seemed so strong. I looked quickly up at his face and saw a pair of green eyes. They were watching me, so I turned my eyes away again. The man continued. He seemed to forget what he was saying earlier.

'If a boy talks to girls or has a girlfriend, I'll hit him. He must not talk to girls. If he has a girlfriend and lies about it, I'll hit him harder than ever.'

He described this to me in a low voice, like a man telling a secret. He was almost warm towards me. He wanted me to understand him.

I waited until he stopped talking. Then I suddenly stood up. I was very worried but I did not want him to know that, so I tied my shoes carefully.

'I must go,' I said. 'Good-day.'

I walked across the field and did not look back.

'Murphy!' I called loudly. I wanted to look brave, but my voice was weak. I called again and Mahony saw me. He shouted a reply and ran towards me. I needed him now. And I was sorry, because I did not always think the best of him.

Eveline

She sat at the window one evening and looked out at the empty street. She was tired. A man walked past to one of the new red houses. There was a field there at one time, and all the children in the street played together in the field. Then a man from Belfast bought it and built houses on it – not like their little brown houses, but bright houses with shining roofs. Her father was not so bad in those days, and her mother was still alive. They were all quite happy. Now most of her brothers and sisters were grown up, her mother was dead, and she was planning to go away too, to leave her home.

Home! She looked round the room at the things that she cleaned once a week. Was it wise to go? At home she had food, a bed, friends and neighbours. Of course she had to work hard, both in the house and in the shop. She was not at all unhappy about leaving the shop, and plenty of other people needed her job.

Her new home was a long way away in an unknown country. She thought about **life** with new friends and without her father's **violence**. He did not hit her in the way that he hit her brothers, but he got angry every Saturday night when she asked for money to buy food, and she was afraid of him. She gave all *her* money, and her brother Harry sent some too, but it was difficult to get any from her father. When he did give her some, she had to hurry to buy Sunday's dinner before the shops closed. Then she returned home late, carrying her heavy bags. She also had to cook, clean, and look after the two youngest children. It was hard work – a hard life – but now she was planning to leave, and all this did not seem quite so terrible.

She thought about her new life in Buenos Aires, her new life with Frank in the home that was waiting for them. She could remember their first meeting so clearly. She was visiting friends

The two letters in her hand were slowly turning grey. One of them was to her brother Harry; Ernest was her favourite, but she liked Harry too.

and he was standing outside the house. His hat sat on the back of his head and his hair fell untidily over his brown face. They had a short conversation in the street.

Every evening after that, he met her outside the shop and walked home with her. He was a sailor on holiday in the country of his birth. He told her about his ships and about his visits to foreign countries. He told her about his place in Buenos Aires. He took her to a musical and she enjoyed sitting in the more expensive part of the theatre. He liked music and he could sing a little. When he sang about the girl who loves a sailor, she felt both uncomfortable and happy at the same time.

Of course her father learnt about the two of them, and he was very angry with her. 'I know these sailors,' he said. He was very unpleasant to Frank, so she had to meet her lover secretly.

It was darker now. The two letters in her hand were slowly turning grey. One of them was to her brother Harry; Ernest was her favourite, but she liked Harry too. The other was to her father. Her father was growing old, and sometimes now he was very nice to her. One day, when she was ill, he read her a story. Another day, when their mother was alive, they all went to the Hill of Howth and had lunch on the grass. Her father put on her mother's hat and the children laughed.

There was not much time, but she continued to sit by the window. She thought about her promise to her mother; she must stay and keep the family together for as long as she could. Then she remembered the last night of her poor mother's illness, after many difficult years of worry and sadness, working for her family. She stood up, suddenly frightened. Escape! She must escape! She wanted to live. She wanted Frank to give her life, perhaps love too. She wanted to be happy. Only Frank could save her.

◆

She stood in the crowd at the boat station. He held her hand and spoke to her about the journey, but she could not answer. The

He pushed his way through the doors and started running towards the boat.
'Come!' he shouted.

station was full of soldiers with brown bags. Her face was white and cold, and she was **praying** silently. She saw the boat through the open doors and then she heard its call. Her unhappiness was making her ill. What was the right thing to do?

There was another call from the boat. He pulled at her hand.

'Come!' he said. 'Come!'

No! No! No! It was impossible.

'Eveline! Evvy!'

He pushed his way through the doors and started running towards the boat.

'Come!' he shouted.

People shouted at him to get on, but he still called to her. She watched him without moving, like a helpless animal. Her eyes showed no love for him, no feeling at all. She did not seem to know that he was there.

The Boarding House

Mrs Mooney was a butcher's daughter. She was a strong woman. She married a man who worked for her father, but after her father died her husband started drinking and taking money from the shop. He fought with her in front of the customers and sold bad meat. One night he ran after her with a large knife and she had to sleep in a neighbour's house.

After that they did not live together any more. Mrs Mooney took the children and the rest of the money from the butcher's business and started a **boarding house** in Hardwicke Street. Tourists came to stay, and sometimes musicians, but most of the visitors were workers from the city.

These young men lived and ate in her house. They liked the same things and were very friendly with each other. They talked about horses and sang songs in the front room on Sunday nights. Polly Mooney, the daughter of the house, sang with them.

Polly was nineteen. She was a thin girl with light soft hair and a small full mouth. Her eyes were grey and green and they looked up at the ceiling when she spoke with anyone. Her mother gave her housework to do so that she could meet the young men. She enjoyed talking to them, but Mrs Mooney knew that none of them was serious. She was beginning to think that Polly must get an office job, when she noticed something between Polly and one of the young men. She watched them carefully.

Polly knew that her mother was watching, and she understood why her mother stayed silent. People in the house began to talk, but Mrs Mooney did nothing. Then at last she made a decision.

It was a bright Sunday morning of early summer. All the windows of the boarding house were open. Outside, people with serious faces and small books in their hands were crossing the square to the church. There were dirty plates on the table of the breakfast-room. Mrs Mooney sat and watched while the servant,

Mr Doran was finding it difficult to shave. His hand was shaking. Dublin was a small city and people in the house already knew about Polly and himself.

Mary, took away the breakfast things. She thought about her conversation with Polly the night before. Polly seemed uncomfortable with her mother's questions but open in her answers.

Mrs Mooney looked at the little clock above the fireplace. It was seventeen minutes past eleven. She must speak to Mr Doran now. He was thirty-four or thirty-five years of age, and Polly was a young girl. He must pay for his enjoyment, but money was not enough. They must get married.

Mr Doran was finding it difficult to shave. His hand was shaking. Dublin was a small city and people in the house already knew about Polly and himself. He had to think about his good name – and his job. He was afraid of his boss. He could almost hear old Mr Leonard's voice: '*Send Mr Doran here, please.*'

He was throwing away years of hard work. He had a little

money; that was not a problem. But people thought badly of her father, and her mother's boarding house did not have a good name. And her English was poor. His friends laughed at her. He could not decide if he liked her or not. He wanted to stay free, not to get married.

While he was sitting on the side of the bed, she knocked and came in. She told him about her conversation with her mother. Her mother knew and wanted to speak with him. She cried and threw her arms around his neck, saying:

'Oh, Bob! Bob! What can I do? What can I do? I want to end it all!'

He told her not to cry. He could feel that she was really afraid.

He heard her again outside his door that first time, late one night. He could still see her in her night clothes. He could smell her skin. After that, every night, when he came home late, she gave him his dinner while the others slept. She was always kind to him. Perhaps they could be happy together …

No, it was not possible. He repeated her words to himself:

'What can I do?'

While he was sitting with her on the side of the bed, Mary came to the door. Mrs Mooney wanted to see him. He stood up and put on his coat.

'Don't worry. It will be all right,' he said quietly.

He left her crying on the bed.

As he went downstairs, he wanted to fly up through the roof and away to another country, but he could not escape the serious faces of Mr Leonard and Mrs Mooney. He walked past Jack Mooney and they said hello coldly. Bob looked at his hard face and his strong body. He remembered a night in the sitting room; a visitor said something about Polly and Jack shouted at him. Nobody played games with *his* sister, he told the visitor. Nobody.

Polly sat for a little time on the side of the bed, crying. Then she dried her eyes and looked in the mirror. She washed her eyes in cold water and made her hair look tidy. Then she sat down on the bed again. She remembered secret, pleasant times in that bed.

She waited, unworried, thinking about the future. Her picture of the future was so clear that she forgot everything around her.

There was no unhappiness in her face now.

She waited, unworried, thinking about the **future**. Her picture of the future was so clear that she forgot everything around her.

At last she heard her mother's voice. She got up and ran to the stairs.

'Polly! Polly!'

'Yes, Mamma?'

'Come down, dear. Mr Doran wants to speak to you.'

Then she remembered.

Counterparts

There was an angry shout from upstairs. When Miss Parker went to the door, the voice called down:

'Send Farrington here!'

Miss Parker returned to her machine. She looked at a man who was writing at a desk.

'Mr Alleyne wants you upstairs.'

The man did not look happy. He pushed back his chair. When he stood up, he was tall and heavy. He had a dark face and a fair moustache. The whites of his eyes were dirty. He walked past the customers, out of the office and up the stairs. On the second floor he stopped outside a door with the name *Mr Alleyne* on it. He knocked. The voice called again:

'Come in!'

The man went into Mr Alleyne's room. Mr Alleyne lifted his pink head, shining like a large egg, from a mountain of papers. Mr Alleyne did not lose a minute.

'Farrington? What is the meaning of this? Where is the **copy** of the **contract** between Bodley and Kirwan? I need it now.'

'*Mr Shelly said, sir...*'

'Listen to me, not to Mr Shelly. You just don't work hard enough, do you! I want that contract before this evening or I'll speak to Mr Crosbie. Do you hear me now?'

'Yes, sir.'

Mr Alleyne looked down at his papers. The man looked angrily at his head. He realised that he was thirsty and felt that he must have a good night's drinking. He could finish the work and then ask Mr Alleyne for some of next month's money. Mr Alleyne's head shot up again saying:

'Eh? Are you going to stand there all day?'

'I was waiting to see ...'

'You needn't wait to see. Go downstairs and do your work.'

He started to write, but at five o'clock he still had five more pages to copy. He got angry and made mistakes.

The man returned to his desk and took up his pen. He looked at the last words on his paper. He was thirsty. He stood up and walked out of the office again. The other workers watched him but said nothing. Outside, he ran quickly down the stairs and along the street to O'Neill's shop. He shouted for a drink and drank it to the bottom. Then, while darkness was falling, he walked back to the office.

'Mr Alleyne was calling for you. Where were you? Five times in one day is a bit ... Well, he wants the Delacour letters.'

The man sat down. He realized that he could not finish his copy of the contract before half past five. He got out the Delacour letters, but he knew that two of them were not there. He took the letters to Mr Alleyne's room and then returned to his desk. He started to write, but at five o'clock he still had five more pages to copy. He got angry and made mistakes. Who could he ask for money? He was ready to meet the boys: Leonard and O'Halloran and Nosey Flynn.

He heard his name. Mr Alleyne was standing next to his desk and shouting at him.

'I know nothing about any other two letters,' the man said.

'*You – know – nothing*. Of course you know nothing,' said Mr Alleyne. 'Do you think I am stupid?'

'I don't think, sir,' the man answered, 'that that's a very clever question to ask me.'

The room fell silent. Mr Alleyne's face turned a deep red. His mouth moved, but at first he was too angry to speak.

'You wait! You'll say that you're sorry or you'll leave this office! You'll leave or you'll tell me that you're sorry!'

The man had to say he was sorry. There were new problems for him in the office now, he knew. It was stupid to speak like that. He wanted to be in the pub, but he needed money.

◆

Outside in the cold, his fingers rested on his watch. Of course! He walked along a narrow street to Terry Kelly's shop, gave him his watch and took the money. When he left, he was feeling happier.

Nosey Flynn was sitting in his usual corner of the pub. When he heard Farrington's story, he bought him a drink. Then Farrington bought a drink. A little later, O'Halloran and Paddy Leonard came in and he told them the story. O'Halloran bought some drinks. Then Farrington bought some more. Higgins came in and Farrington told him his story again. They all laughed loudly.

They left the pub and walked towards the city. Rain was falling on the cold streets so they had another drink at the Scotch House, and then another. A man called Weathers promised to show them some nice girls. O'Halloran said that he and Leonard could go but that Farrington was a married man. Farrington found this amusing. Weathers bought them

When her group was leaving the room, she knocked against his chair and said Oh, pardon! *in a voice that was English.*

one more drink and then they went round to Mulligan's.

O'Halloran ordered the pub's special hot drinks, and Farrington ordered some more. They had little money now, but there was just enough. Two young women with big hats and a young man in a suit came in. One of the women caught Farrington's eye. She looked at him with her large dark brown eyes. When her group was leaving the room, she knocked against his chair and said *Oh, pardon!* in a voice that was English. He watched her leave, but she did not look back at him. He was angry that he had no more money.

He stood at the corner of O'Connell Bridge. He was unhappy and still angry; he still did not feel **drunk** and he had only twopence in his pocket. He had problems at the office, he was without his watch, he had no money, and he was not drunk. He began to feel thirsty again and he wanted to be back in the hot, smelly pub. He thought about the woman in the big hat knocking against him and saying *Pardon!* and he felt more and more angry.

He caught the bus to Shelbourne Road. He never liked returning home. When he went in, the kitchen was empty and the fire was dying. He shouted upstairs:

'Ada! Ada!'

A little boy came running down the stairs.

'Who is that?' said the man, looking through the darkness.

'Me, Pa.'

'Who are you? Charlie?'

'No, Pa. Tom.'

'Where's your mother?'

'She's out at church.'

'That's right … Did she think of leaving any dinner for me?'

'Yes, Pa. I …'

'Light the lamp. Why is it dark? Are the other children in bed?'

The man sat down heavily on one of the chairs. When the room was light, he hit the table with his hand and shouted:

'What's for my dinner?'

'I'll cook it now, Pa,' said the little boy.

The man jumped up and pointed to the fire.

'On *that* fire? The fire's gone out! You didn't watch it! I'll teach you to do that again!'

He picked up a walking stick from behind the door. The little boy ran round the table. He was crying. The man followed him and caught him by his coat. The little boy could see no escape and fell on his knees.

'Next time you'll watch the fire!' said the man, hitting him hard. The boy screamed as the stick cut his leg.

'O, Pa! Don't hit me, Pa! I'll pray for you … Don't hit me …'

A Painful Case

Mr James Duffy lived in Chapelizod because he wanted to live as far as possible from the centre of Dublin and from the more modern parts of the city. He lived in an old, dark house. Through his windows he could see Dublin's shallow river and factories that closed long ago. There was little furniture in his room, no pictures and nothing on the floor. But there were plenty of books on the walls and there were papers on his desk. He wrote a sentence or two in those papers from time to time when an interesting thought came to him.

Mr Duffy's face, not young any more, was the brown colour of the Dublin streets. Dry black hair grew on his long and quite large head. Below his moustache was a hard, unfriendly mouth, but his eyes were sad and not unkind. They seemed to look for good in others, but he watched and thought about himself in the way that he thought about strangers, never quite sure about the things that he did. He never gave money to people in the street, and he walked quickly with a strong stick, like a man with purpose in his life.

He worked in a bank in Baggot Street until four o'clock every day. After work he had dinner in an eating-house and then travelled home. Sometimes he went out again to listen to music. He had no friends and no church. From time to time he thought about robbing the bank, but it never seemed a very sensible idea.

One evening he was at a **concert**. The room was nearly empty and a woman began to talk to him. She was with her daughter and was perhaps a few years younger than him. She had a strong, intelligent face and very calm, dark blue eyes. Her name was Mrs Sinico and her husband was a ship's **captain**. He met her at another concert a few weeks later, and many times after that –

He met her at another concert a few weeks later, and many times after that – always in the evening.

always in the evening. At first they walked together, but Mr Duffy was uncomfortable with secrets and finally she asked him to her house. Captain Sinico was happy about his visits, thinking they were to his daughter. Since *he* did not notice his wife in that way, it did not seem possible that another man could.

The husband was often away and the daughter out giving music lessons, so Mr Duffy enjoyed a lot of time with the woman. Adventures like this were new to both of them, and neither he nor she found it at all strange. He brought her his books and gave her his ideas. She listened carefully to everything he said. Sometimes she told him some facts of her life. In a motherly way she tried to teach him to live and to feel in a more natural way.

He often went to her little country house outside Dublin, and

She took his hand in excitement and pulled it to her face.
Mr Duffy was very much surprised.

they came to know each other in the dark evenings. He grew warm and happy, and talked to her about the great problems of life. She listened with bright eyes, and then one day, when he finished talking, she took his hand in excitement and pulled it to her face.

Mr Duffy was very much surprised. It was suddenly clear to him that she did not understand the *seriousness* of his words. He did not visit her for a week; then he wrote to her, asking her to meet him. They met in a cake shop near the Parkgate and walked up and down the roads of the park for nearly three hours. They agreed not to meet again. When they came out of the park, they walked silently towards the bus; but here she began to shake so much that he said goodbye quickly and left her. A few days later she sent him back his books and music.

Four years went past. Mr Duffy returned to his usual way of life. He bought some new books, but he wrote no more than a few lines in the papers on his desk. One sentence read: Love between man and man is not possible because there must be no **sex**; man and woman cannot be friends because there must be sex. He stayed away from concerts so that he did not meet her by accident. His father died. And still every morning he went to work in the city, and every evening he walked home after having his dinner in the eating-house with the evening paper.

One evening, while he was eating, his hand stopped on its way to his mouth. His eyes rested on a piece of news in the paper. He put his fork back on his plate and read. Then he drank some water and read it again. His food began to get cold. The girl came and asked about his dinner. Was there something wrong with it? It was very good, he said, and ate a little. Then he paid his bill and went out.

When he arrived home, he took the newspaper out of his pocket and read the page again.

WOMAN DIES AT SYDNEY PARADE
A PAINFUL CASE

Mrs Emily Sinico, forty-three years of age, died at Sydney Parade Station yesterday. The ten o'clock slow train from Kingstown hit her while she was trying to cross the line. The police have talked to railway workers; Mrs Sinico often crossed the lines from platform to platform late at night, and there was nothing that the driver of the train could do. The dead woman's husband, Captain Sinico, of Leoville, Sydney Parade, was not in Dublin at the time of the accident, since he was travelling home from Rotterdam. He and his wife were happily married for twenty years until two years ago when Mrs Sinico turned to drink.

Mr Duffy lifted his eyes from the paper and looked out of the window. Night was falling over the river. What an end! He had strong feelings about it. Talking to her about important, personal matters was clearly a serious mistake. Her name was black and now he felt dirty too. His friend, carrying empty bottles to the bar for more drink like so many street people! Oh, what an end! He was happy not to know her now.

He felt ill. He put on his coat and hat quickly and went out. When he came to the pub at Chapelizod Bridge, he went in and ordered a drink. He sat there for a long time, thinking about his life with her. Slowly he realized that she was dead. He began to feel more and more uncomfortable. He finally understood the **loneliness** of her life. Nobody was interested in him; *he* was **lonely** too.

It was after nine o'clock when he left the pub. The night was cold. He walked in the park, and she seemed to be near him. He could feel her voice touch his ear, her hand touch his. He stood still and listened. Why did he leave her to die?

He walked in the park, and she seemed to be near him. He could feel her voice touch his ear, her hand touch his.

He stopped on top of Magazine Hill and looked towards Dublin. Below him he noticed the shapes of people lying together. He felt terribly unhappy. She loved him and he turned his back on her. She was dead and he could not enjoy life in the way that other people did. The shapes in the darkness wanted him to go away. Nobody wanted him.

He looked over at the river and saw the lights of a train moving slowly through the darkness. The noise of the train repeated the sound of her name. Then everything fell silent. He could not hear her or feel her. He waited for a few minutes, but there was nothing. There was nobody there.

The Dead

Lily had too much to do. Each time she brought one man into the house and took his coat, another visitor arrived at the door. Luckily she did not have to worry about the women. Miss Kate and Miss Julia were showing them upstairs to a bathroom in which they could change.

Everybody who knew the Misses Morkan, or their **niece** Mary Jane, came each year to their dance – family, old friends, people who Julia sang with, some of Kate's older piano students. The dance always went well.

But the women of the house were worried now. It was after ten o'clock and Gabriel and his wife were not there. They were also worried about Freddy Malins: he was not there either, and he always drank too much before he came. Every two minutes one of the two women called down to Lily: Was Gabriel or Freddy there yet?

'Oh, Mr Conroy,' said Lily to Gabriel, when she opened the door to him. 'Here you are. Good evening, Mrs Conroy.'

'The problem is,' said Gabriel, 'that my wife takes three hours to dress herself.'

Lily called Kate and Julia, and they hurried down the stairs. They kissed Gabriel's wife, and the three women went upstairs. Lily took Gabriel's coat and shook off the snow.

'Is it snowing again, Mr Conroy?' asked Lily.

Gabriel looked at her and smiled. She was a thin, growing girl with a white face. She did the housework for his aunts and his cousin. He remembered Lily when she was a child, sitting silently on the stairs while her father worked in the house.

'Yes, Lily,' he answered. 'It's a cold night out there.'

He watched her while she carefully put away his coat.

'Tell me, Lily,' he said in a friendly voice, 'do you still go to school?'

'Oh, Mr Conroy,' said Lily to Gabriel when she opened the door to him.
'Here you are. Good evening, Mrs Conroy.'

'Oh no, sir, not now,' she answered.

'Oh, then,' said Gabriel, 'I hope to be at your wedding soon.'

The girl looked at him. Her voice, when she spoke, was angry.

'Men now are only interested in talking and in what they can get from you!'

Gabriel went red. He wanted to be kind, but his words were clearly a mistake. He cleaned his shoes and then, without looking at her, took some money from his pocket.

'Oh, Lily,' he said, putting it into her hands, 'it's Christmas time, isn't it? Just … here's a little …'

He walked quickly towards the stairs.

'Oh, no, sir!' called the girl, following him. 'Really, sir, I can't take it …'

'Christmas time! Christmas time!' said Gabriel, almost running up the stairs.

'Well, thank you, sir.'

He waited outside the sitting room door for the dance to end. He was still unhappy about Lily's angry words. He took a piece of paper from his pocket and looked quickly at his **speech**. He was not sure about the lines from Robert Browning; they were perhaps a little difficult for his listeners, and he did not want to make another mistake. Just then his aunts and his wife came out of the dressing-room. The old women kissed Gabriel warmly. They liked the son of their dead sister, Ellen. They talked a little about his plans and about the cold weather. Then Julia looked down the stairs.

'Here's Freddy,' she said.

At the same moment the dancing stopped. The sitting room door opened and a few people came out.

'Go down, Gabriel, and see if he's all right. Don't bring him up if he's drunk. I'm sure he's drunk. I'm sure he is,' Aunt Kate said to Gabriel in a low voice.

Gabriel went downstairs and the others went into the back room. There were tables of food and drink. Some young men were drinking beer. The women asked for lemonade. Mary Jane was bringing people together for the next dance. The piano began to play in the sitting room and most people followed her in. Then Aunt Julia came slowly into the back room.

'What's the matter, Julia?' asked Aunt Kate, looking worried. 'Who is it?'

Julia turned to her sister. The question seemed to surprise her.

'It's only Freddy, Kate, and Gabriel with him.'

Freddy Malins was laughing loudly at a story that he was telling Gabriel.

'Good evening, Freddy,' said Aunt Julia.

Freddy said good evening and immediately found another visitor to tell his story to.

'He's not so bad, is he?' said Aunt Kate to Gabriel.

'Oh no, it doesn't really show ...'

◆

Gabriel could not listen while Mary Jane played the piano to the silent crowd. He did not like the music; in fact only Mary Jane herself and Aunt Kate seemed very interested. He looked around the room and his eyes rested on a picture of his mother, a proud and serious woman. His mother did not like Gretta, the woman that he married. She called her 'a sweet girl from the country', but Gretta was not a country girl. It was Gretta who looked after his mother during her last long illness.

Mary Jane finished playing and Gabriel found himself with Miss Ivors for the next dance. Miss Ivors was a young woman with honest brown eyes who talked a lot. She and Gabriel were friends at university and they were both teachers, so they knew each other well. When they took their places, she said:

'Mr Conroy, will you come to the Aran Isles this summer? We're going to stay there a month. Mr Clancy is coming, and Mr Kilkelly and Kathleen Kearney. Gretta will enjoy it. She's from Connacht, isn't she?'

'Her people are,' said Gabriel shortly.

'Well, we usually go to France or Belgium or perhaps Germany,' said Gabriel, feeling less and less comfortable.

'But you will come, won't you?' said Miss Ivors, putting her warm hand on his arm.

'The problem is,' said Gabriel, 'I'm going …'

'Going where?' asked Miss Ivors.

'Well, you know, every year some friends and I go on a bicycle tour …'

'But where?' asked Miss Ivors.

'Well, we usually go to France or Belgium or perhaps Germany,' said Gabriel, feeling less and less comfortable.

'And why do you go to France and Belgium,' said Miss Ivors, 'instead of visiting *your* country?'

'Well,' said Gabriel, 'it's partly to practise the languages and partly for a change.'

'And what about practising *your* language – Irish?' said Miss Ivors.

'Well,' said Gabriel, 'in fact, you know, Irish is not my language.'

Their neighbours on the dance floor were listening to this conversation and Gabriel was turning red while at the same time he tried hard to sound pleasant.

'And what about visiting *your* country,' continued Miss Ivors, 'and your people? You know nothing of them.'

'Oh, really,' Gabriel replied suddenly. 'I'm sick of my country, sick of it.'

'Why?' asked Miss Ivors. Gabriel did not answer. 'Why?' she repeated. 'Of course, you've no answer.'

Gabriel danced without looking at her, but when the lines of dancers met again she pressed his hand and looked at him until he smiled.

After the dance, Gabriel spoke to Freddy Malins's mother. He tried to forget the conversation with Miss Ivors. Then the family and close friends sat down to supper, with Gabriel at the head of the table. They could hear the music and the women's skirts on the floor above them. Gabriel cut the meat and Lily took round the hot potatoes. Aunt Kate and Aunt Julia opened bottles of beer and soft drinks. The room grew noisy with people talking and laughing and the sounds of knives and forks. They talked about music, about the great singer Caruso, and about other singers of the past. At last Gabriel's wife put sweets and fruit on the table. The room fell silent when Gabriel pushed back his chair and stood up.

He rested his shaking fingers on the table and smiled. Then he began:

'I am not a good speaker, but I am very pleased to be able to talk to you now about my warm feelings for three good women.'

Everybody laughed or smiled at Aunt Kate and Aunt Julia and Mary Jane. They all turned a little red. Gabriel continued:

'We are right to be proud of the way we, in this country, look after our visitors. And the kind, unselfish welcome that the women in *this* house offer their visitors is a shining example of the

Irish way. Sometimes I am afraid that young people, with their new ideas, seem to forget what is truly important. Let us remember those who are dead while we also continue to work bravely among the living. Here we are friends and music lovers, and lovers too of these three great women. So let us drink to them now!'

Each of the visitors stood up, glass in hand. Gabriel looked down at his aunts. Aunt Julia was smiling; Aunt Kate was crying into her handkerchief.

◆

The last visitors stood by the front door. Each time it opened, the cold morning air blew into the house. Gabriel put his coat on and looked around.

'Is Gretta not down yet?'

'She's getting her things,' said Aunt Kate.

Mary Jane looked at him.

'I feel cold just looking at you in those heavy clothes,' she said. 'What a terrible time to travel home.'

While the others stayed by the door talking, Gabriel went to the bottom of the stairs and looked up. A woman stood in the shadow near the top. He could not see her face, but he could see her skirt. It was his wife. She was quite still, and she was listening to something. Gabriel tried to hear too. A piano was playing softly and a man was singing.

Aunt Kate, Aunt Julia and Mary Jane came towards him laughing. Gabriel pointed at his wife and asked them with his hand to be silent. The song was an Irish one, a song of unhappy love, of a dead lover.

'Oh,' said Mary Jane. 'It's Bartell D'Arcy. He didn't want to sing earlier. I'll ask him to sing another song for us.'

'Oh, do that, Mary Jane,' said Aunt Kate.

Mary Jane hurried upstairs, but the singing suddenly stopped and they heard the sound of the piano closing.

'Oh, what a pity!' said Mary Jane.

She was quite still, and she was listening to something. Gabriel tried to hear too. A piano was playing softly and a man was singing.

Gabriel watched his wife, standing silently. At last she turned towards them and Gabriel saw the colour in her face and her shining eyes. Suddenly he felt very happy.

They all went to the door.

'Well, good-night, Aunt Kate, and thanks for the pleasant evening.'

'Good-night, Gabriel. Good-night, Gretta.'

'Good-night, Aunt Kate, and thanks. Good-night, Aunt Julia.'

'Good-night, Miss Morkan.'

'Good-night. Good-night.'

The morning was still dark. She walked in front of him with Mr Bartell D'Arcy, holding her skirt up out of the snow. Gabriel's eyes were still bright with happiness. He wanted to run after her and say something loving. He wanted to forget the ordinariness of their years together and remember only the happy times.

They found a taxi. She looked out of the window and seemed tired. When they got out at their hotel, he touched her arm. He was almost shaking, he needed to hold her against him so badly. In the room he watched her undress.

'Gretta!'

She walked towards him. Her face looked serious.

'Do you feel ill?'

'No, tired, that's all.'

She stood by the window, looking out. She seemed a long way away. Then she turned and kissed him. Gabriel put his hands on her hair. His heart was full of happiness because she came to him. He held her and said softly:

'Gretta, what are you thinking about?'

She did not answer at once. Then she started crying.

'Oh, I am thinking about that song. The one that Mr D'Arcy played.'

She ran to the bed and hid her face. Gabriel followed her.

'What about the song? Why are you crying? Why, Gretta?'

'I knew a person a long time ago who sang that song.'

'And who was that person long ago?' asked Gabriel, smiling.

'It was a person I knew in Galway when I lived with my grandmother,' she said.

Gabriel's face lost its smile.

'Somebody that you were in love with?' he asked.

'A young boy called Michael Furey. He sang that song. He was a very weak child with big dark eyes.'

'You were in love with him?' said Gabriel, beginning to feel angry.

'I walked with him,' she said, 'when I was in Galway. He's dead. He died when he was only seventeen. Isn't it a terrible thing to die so young?'

While Gabriel was thinking of his secret life with his wife, she was thinking of another. He felt very uncomfortable.

'Were you in love with Michael Furey, Gretta?' he said.

'At that time, very much, yes,' she said.

Her voice was sad. Gabriel realized that he must forget his plans for the night. He took one of her hands and said, also sadly:

'And what did he die of so young, Gretta?'

'I think he died for me,' she answered. Gabriel felt more and more unhappy. 'He was ill when I left my grandmother's to come here. They didn't want me to see him so I wrote him a letter. That night I heard stones against the window. I ran downstairs and he was out there in the rain, shaking with cold.'

'And did you not tell him to go back?' asked Gabriel.

'I told him to go home immediately. But he was so sad. He didn't want to live. I can see his eyes now.'

'And did he go home?'

'Yes, he went home. And a week later he died. Oh, the day they told me!'

She stopped and threw herself down on the bed, crying. Gabriel held her hand for a moment, and then left her and walked quietly to the window.

♦

She was asleep. Gabriel lay on the bed and watched her. A

He thought of the woman next to him and the secret she carried in her heart. He felt great love for her.

man died for her. She was probably a very beautiful girl, but her face now was not the one that Michael Furey died for.

He thought about his feelings earlier, how strong they were. Why was that? Because of his aunts' supper, his speech, the wine and dancing, the walk in the snow. Poor Aunt Julia! She was old now. She did not have long to live. One after the other people all became shadows. Better to go bravely when you were strong than to grow old and weak.

He thought of the woman next to him and the secret she carried in her heart. He felt great love for her. He saw again her lover standing in the rain. He looked out of the window. Snow was falling again. It was time, he thought sleepily, to travel west. Yes, the newspapers were right: snow was falling in every part of Ireland. It was falling too on Michael Furey. It was falling everywhere, it seemed for the last time, on the living and the dead.

EXERCISES

Vocabulary Work

Look back at the 'Dictionary Words' in these stories. Make sure that you know the meaning of each word.

1 Find a word which means:
   a *another exactly the same*
   b *a programme of pieces of music*
   c *feeling sad, without other people*
   d *the daughter of your brother or sister*
   e *a kind of hotel*
   f *talking to God*
   g *a written agreement*
2 Use these words to write new sentences, showing the meaning of the words clearly:
   a captain/drunk/stick
   b life/future
   c speech/sex/violence

Comprehension

An Encounter
Here are some of the things the two boys did. Which thing happened first, second, third, etc.? Start with b.

a They talked to an old man.
b They went to the big river.
c One boy ran away and threw stones at a cat.
d They crossed the river in a boat.
e The other boy got frightened and left the old man.
f They lay and rested in a field.
g They bought pink lemonade.

Eveline

Eveline didn't leave with Frank on the boat to South America. Why do you think she stayed in Dublin?

The Boarding House

All these people live in the boarding house. What are their names?

a The woman who bought the house.

b The woman's daughter.

c Her son, with 'a hard face and a strong body.'

d A man of about 35, interested in the girl.

Counterparts

1 How did Farrington get money to pay for his drinks?

2 His son Tom did something wrong and so his father hit him. What was Tom's mistake?

A Painful Case

Mr Duffy and Mrs Sinico were good friends. Suddenly they stopped meeting. What happened that changed everything between them?

The Dead

1 Finish the sentences below about the family in this story.

Kate Morkan is Julia's *sister*.

a Mary Jane is Kate and Julia's . . .

b Ellen was Kate and Julia's . . .

c Gabriel Conroy is Ellen's . . .

d Gretta is Gabriel's . . .

2 Gabriel talked with Miss Ivors but they didn't agree about something. What was it?

3 Why did Gretta feel so sad when she remembered Michael Furey?

Discussion

1 Many of the people in these stories are very unhappy: Eveline, Bob Doran, Mr Farrington, Mrs Sinico, Mr Duffy. What makes them unhappy? The same things or different things?

2 Mr Farrington seems to be three different people: when he is in the

office; when he is in the pubs with his friends; and when he goes home. Why is this?

3 These stories show Dublin life around 1914. What did people then do in their free time? What do you think they do today?

Writing

1 Choose one of the pictures in this book. Write about the people in the picture: their names, how they look, what they are doing and what they are thinking (100–150 words).

2 You are Mr Alleyne in *Counterparts*. Write a letter to Mr Farrington, saying that he has lost his job in your business. Explain why.

3 You are Julia Morkan in *The Dead*. Write to a cousin in America telling her about your Christmas party, and the people in your family who were at the party.

Review

1 Which story did you enjoy most? Say why.

2 Which story was the most difficult to understand? Why was it difficult?